THE
DIALOGUE

THE DIALOGUE

Ridding the World of the Scourge of Wars

BYRON DARING

iUniverse, Inc.
Bloomington

The Dialogue
Ridding the World of the Scourge of Wars

iUniverse books may be ordered through booksellers or by contacting:

iUniverse
1663 Liberty Drive
Bloomington, IN 47403
www.iuniverse.com
1-800-Authors (1-800-288-4677)

ISBN: 978-1-4759-3129-7 (sc)
ISBN: 978-1-4759-3131-0 (ebk)

Printed in the United States of America

iUniverse rev. date: 07/26/2012

CONTENTS

A NOTE FROM THE AUTHOR

This book was inspired from a burning desire to address the futility of wars.

When traveling around the world, we can admire the beauty of this unique planet and meet people of different nationalities, cultures, and expectations.

Most reasonable people enjoy and thrive on peaceful living. The antithesis is war. I have witnessed injured soldiers and civilians and emotionally devastated children and adults who are victims of wars.

If peace is so wonderful, what are the causes of its loss?

How can we engage in conflict resolutions with rational polemics?

These are the reasons and questions that inspired me to write this book.

The event that led to this project was the escalation of the war from Iraq to Afghanistan, and the possible extension of wars through the Middle East and Africa.

The main purpose of this work is to review the historical, religious, social, economic, and medical aspects or wars.

Through the dialogue between two English-speaking enemy soldiers, the similarities in principles and the differences which can be reconciled become evident.

CHAPTER 1

Tragic Encounter of a Military Convoy in Afghanistan

Fighter jets blanket the sky. F-14 Tomcats do the grunt work, pounding the enemy and weakening his resolve. F-15 Eagles add stealthy, tactical support, further disorienting their ragtag, but highly-trained, troops. Smoke from the Taliban's RPG7s and 82mm mortars, as well as the ISAF's Humvees and Bradleys, writhe together in an acrid and poisonous mélange. Dust from all this activity regularly clogs the motors and turbines of the multivariate war machines, impeding swift and efficient progress. It is slow going, and any real and lasting success seems, at best, illusory. Still, the convoy presses on. A jet precedes them, detonating the underground bombs and ordnance in their path. Despite this strategy, as the convoy negotiates a turn a series of IEDs explode and several Humvees are destroyed.

First Lieutenant John Wagner and his junior officer brother, Peter, are amongst the casualties. In a phantasmagoria of semiconscious and unconscious stupor, John discerns the fleeting image of Peter regarding him with fraternal concern. Only when he finally regains full consciousness does he discover his brother's bloody corpse. Sensing his shaky equilibrium, he rushes into the nearby mountains and takes cover in a ditch. He clenches his MP5 submachine gun tightly and realizes it is jammed.

"Damn it. Damn it. Damn this place to hell." He suppresses his seething rage in a hiss.

Unbeknownst to John, a Taliban fighter by the name of Abdullah Gul is sheltering in a cave above and behind the ditch he is hiding in.

Left by himself, John is not only aware of the loss of his only sibling, but also the realization that this conflict has become his own personal war. He grew up hearing his father's stories of the Great War, and it had always seemed very real to him and his brother. But the truth was that all that happened a long time ago, and the intervening years had buried it. This war was here and now, and it belonged to Peter and him. Now it only belonged to him.

Poor Peter of the bright, sapphire eyes and dark mane, so like a medieval knight in appearance. John recalled his enthusiasm upon hearing of the new XM 25 rifle. It represented the cutting edge of American technology, a shoulder-fired weapon with a 25 mm load. Each unit cost $35,000 and fired a projectile with a computer chip embedded in it. A button on the side could incrementally add meters to the target range. Anything or anyone near its intended scope would be neutralized.

"This is the great equalizer, Johnny boy. I don't care what rabbit hole the target tries to hide in. They can't scurry fast enough before they get tagged."

In his coltish excitement, John remembered the breathless intensity his kid brother displayed when they played cowboys and Indians as little children. Even when their mother would call them in to supper, Peter seemed to still be lost in the game. It was as if the normal course of mundane life was just too boring for him. He probably would have been happy as a hero in a Sir Walter Scott novel. He would win the day by a combination of peerless skill and superior weaponry. He was just as anachronistic as his appearance.

Wars are no longer won through sophisticated technology. Wars are won in the hearts of the men who fight them. In today's landscape of protracted guerilla skirmishes and campaigns of attrition, there is no room for the military caricatures so popular in the past. This is particularly the case in a country like Afghanistan.

Afghanistan is slightly smaller than Texas. It has arid plains and high mountains because of the abundance of minerals, which according some authors, are "the best bet for beating opium". The country could be transformed into one of the world's mining centers.

The geography of this mountainous and rugged country makes fighting the enemy exceedingly difficult. Air bombs are useless unless they block the entrances to the caves the rebels often use for cover. Low-flying planes are vulnerable to strikes from surface-to-air missiles, mortars, and even machine gun fire. Convoys transit through tortuous, narrow roads that leave them prey to sudden rebel attacks and buried IEDs. This is the very reason that Afghanistan has so successfully resisted invaders even in modern times, when its people have faced advanced weaponry. Small groups of rebels are difficult to find and destroy. In addition, terror also acts as a disincentive. When members of the alliance forces are killed, their decapitated heads are often displayed, with or without their helmets, along the roadside to remind soldiers of the dangers and possible outcomes of their presence as invaders.

Wars against enemies fighting in deserts and flat terrains are relatively easy to prosecute, primarily by the use of fighter jets and drones. Ground forces can then sweep through and dominate a much-weakened resistance. On the other hand, wars against small tribal groups who take cover in familiar mountains and are used to Spartan meals and harsh weather conditions, to which invading armies are unaccustomed, are much more difficult to fight.

Human beings are designed to fight for survival. The Taliban are psychologically prepared to resist hunger, dust storms, extreme hot and cold environments, and, most significantly, fear. According to the Islamic religion, when one dies serving Allah and the faith, he will be generously rewarded in paradise.

It is not the same dynamic to defend your own family and country as it is to fight in a foreign land that does not represent an imminent threat, especially when the putative goals seem unjustified. It is well-nigh impossible to change a people's way of living, thinking, and being through war.

John was painfully aware of Afghanistan's land, the Taliban's way of fighting and the difficulty of changing people through war, even in his weakened state. In a state of passive lucidity, John's life flashed back to him, not so much as a frantic recap, but as a series of home movies.

CHAPTER 2

A Brief Biography of
Two Enemy Soldiers

Fall 1987

It was after school. There was a matting of maple leaves that muffled the boys' numerous footfalls. John did not want to fight, but this was one of the more tiresome rituals of boyhood. Troy Green resented that John had not participated in the stealthy pilfering of candy bars from the school cafeteria. In small-town America, conformity is king. Troy decided John was being superior and challenged him to a fight. Normally, John would ignore mere taunts, but now these had escalated into assault. Obviously, Troy did not comprehend restraint. Now that fighting was inevitable, John decided he would wrestle Troy to the ground to avoid any serious damage. He hoped Troy's entourage of cohorts would remain spectators.

Troy approached John. "Who do you think you are, Mr. Goody Two-Shoes?" Troy was posturing, but he was also turning crimson.

John sighed. "Look Troy, cut the crap. It's no big deal. I wasn't going to tattle on you anyway. Let it go."

"Let it go?" Troy tossed his long red bangs to the left side of his head and looked for encouragement from his fans in classic WWE fashion. "What's the matter, John? You some kinda yellow belly?" This was met by yelping derision from the peanut gallery.

John shrugged. "All right. Let's get this over with."

Troy and John circled each other like cautious hyenas. Then like a wild boar, Peter came charging in a cloud of dry autumn leaves.

"You leave my brother alone, or I'll kill you all. I mean it." Peter scanned the playground with menacing eyes. His jugular vein was throbbing, and he was on the verge of tears. John looked pleadingly at his kid brother.

"Peter, please. Let me handle this."

The crowd, which initially found this amusing, became increasingly unsettled. Troy, the consummate entertainer, sensed the shift.

"Whoa. What's this? I didn't know this was a family reunion. What's the matter with your brother anyway, John? He some kinda retard?"

John glared. "Go to hell."

Troy waved his hands in dismissal.

"Nah, man. This is pathetic." He rejoined his schoolmates and left the yard in feigned mirth.

John reassured Peter that all was well. His seriousness and Peter's wildness were both seen as defects by the other, and thus, was a plea for protection.

Spring 1991

John looked around the auditorium and marveled at the tacky décor. Between the tin foil cut outs and the tinsel, it was positively nauseating. But for the pulsating soundtrack of the Pet Shop Boys, Duran Duran, and the other bands of the Second British Invasion, he would have thought he was attending a birthday party at an old folks home. He made his way through the strained laughter to a small group of giggling schoolgirls. Ever since he was a young boy, he had a special sense about girls. He could always tell, no matter how they acted outwardly, which ones truly cared, and which were disingenuous. In addition, some girls shone.

Even in a crowd, they would be bathed in radiance. This was how he knew that Mary Hogan was the one. John had seen her in English class reciting Hamlet's soliloquy, as was required from all the students. She impressed him with her simple, unpretentious demeanor. She seldom wore any makeup, not needing any embellishment to her understated redheaded beauty. Whereas they had already spoken to each other casually, John felt the need for some clarification as to her intentions. Now he approached her and extended his left hand.

"May I have this dance, mademoiselle?"

Mary rose as if she were mounting the podium to accept an Olympic medal. "Mais, naturellment, monsieur. Vous ete tres sympathique."

"Merci." It was all John could think to say in his embarrassed discomfiture.

John and Mary waltzed incongruously to up-tempo tunes that were endemically unromantic. At first this evoked general ridicule from their fellow revelers. But this was followed, shortly thereafter, by belated admiration. They were quite the couple. As she sank her head onto his chest, a bouquet of gardenias rose from her braided tresses. John concentrated on keeping his footing as he found himself adrift.

"I just knew you were the one for me," he whispered hoarsely.

Mary smiled and continued dancing and humming to herself. Then she raised her head to face John.

"I knew too."

"How did you know?"

She framed his head with her uplifted hands.

"I could see it."

Winter 1995

The Mass had ended. The smell of incense lingered, lending a timeless, oriental quality to the rite. As they exited the church, the congregants solemnly boarded the waiting limousines. The tires rolling over the loose gravel sounded like a sad and desultory rain shower. By the time the funeral cortege wound its way through the gently undulating graveyard, John was troubled by an uneasy memory. At the funeral home, when John had approached his mother's casket to pay his last respects, he felt ambivalent. He, of course, knew that his mother no longer resided in that mortal frame that seemed to lie so oblivious to the surrounding mourners. Still, she seemed familiar and approachable, attired as she was in her favorite olive dress. He reached over to tap her cheek in lieu of a kiss, and became petrified. Her face was as solid as steel, apparently the effect of the formaldehyde used in preparing the body. He looked around to see if anyone had noticed his shock. As he looked at the assorted faces in various stereotypical poses, he could not help feeling like a participant in a grotesque masquerade. He had never felt so alone in his life.

Now, in the graveyard, while the minister recited the orations, John remarked his father's urgent stare. Peter was sulking moodily with his face averted from all those gathered, like Judas in some popular renditions of the Last Supper. During the burial, as the family took turns dropping roses on the coffin's lid, Anthony drew John aside. When they were a safe distance from the others, Anthony grabbed John firmly by the shoulders.

"Johnny boy, I'm going to need you to be strong, if only for Pete's sake."

John scowled at his father's halfhearted attempt at humor.

"Seriously, son. Look at me."

John could see that his father's serene blue eyes had taken on a stormy cast.

"Needless to say, your brother was very close to his mother. You were too, but he was her baby. She always felt there was something that was not quite right in the boy, and

I suppose she was right. Still, I don't think mollycoddling him did him any good. I always told her she was spoiling him, but she was stubborn. It's one of the things I loved about her. Now, you know that boy never listened to me upwards of ten seconds without rolling his eyes toward the ceiling. You're the only one who can talk any sense to him. I've been noticing that he's taken to disappearing some nights, and it has me worried sick. I just don't want him running around with the wrong crowd."

John shrugged. "Who am I? My brother's keeper?"

Anthony mockingly remonstrated with his son, extending his right index finger.

"Now, Johnny boy, don't be quoting the world's most notorious fratricide. I'm beginning to think I'm losing you too."

Anthony knew this was not the case. No matter how much John tried to act rebelliously, it simply was not in his nature. He had always been a serious young man. For his part, John did not have the heart to tell his father, the chaplain, that Peter was not horsing around or joyriding, but rather had taken to visiting a house of ill repute in Cedar Rapids. John had gone with Peter once with disguised sangfroid. He did not want Peter to think he was judging him. He wanted to seem objective. And, from a clinical standpoint, he wanted to assess the general health of the staff. Naturally, the painted denizens of that questionable establishment greeted him with exaggerated warmth in their lavish attire. To John, they seemed like the faded queens of an old deck of cards. Still, that was the only thing that seemed to take the edge out of Peter's hurt, if only temporarily. And, of course, there was no danger of falling in love with those sad inhabitants of an alternate universe.

John shrugged his shoulders again as he faced his father, now bathed by the setting sun.

"What can I tell him? You know he has always seen me as a stick-in-the-mud."

Anthony smiled. "I trust you, Johnny boy. You'll know what to do. Remember what Saint Augustine said, 'Love and do what you will.'"

John had joined the ROTC at the University of Iowa, and had been very proud to have been a part of the Mighty Hawkeye Battalion. He reminisced fondly of presenting the colors at the homecoming football game. Kinnick Stadium had been packed that cool and clear day. With a flicker in his heart, he sensed that his girlfriend Mary was watching him. This was not easy, as she herself was busy as a cheerleader. Once their eyes met and she winked coyly, her red hair framing her twinkling chestnut eyes. John felt a tingle like ice cream melting in his head. He felt right then that she would be his future wife.

Spring 1997

John tried not to strut as he greeted the assembled kith and kin who had come to congratulate him. He had graduated with honors and was bedecked in his full dress regalia. Anthony Wagner barreled his way through the crowd and gave his son a hearty bear hug.

"I'm so proud of you, Johnny boy, I could cry."

John snickered. "Please don't, Dad. You'll ruin my uniform."

Anthony shook with laughter and left to welcome the incoming guests.

Peter moodily remarked, "Watch out, Johnny. It's unseasonably warm outside. Your suit might catch fire."

John embraced his brother. "Come on, Peter. Be happy for me."

"All joshing aside, Johnny, you look like an officer and a gentleman. You better have a good speech ready," he said, motioning to the guests. "These folks know you're the preacher's son."

John grabbed Peter by the shoulders. "So are you, Peter. Never forget that. Remember what I told you about all this moral relativism you've been flirting with. It's no good pretending you're any worse than you truly are."

Peter guffawed. "There's a lot of truth in what you say, reverend. Just please don't cast me headlong into eternal perdition."

John smiled. "Seriously, Pete. Remember what Dad always says. It's a spiritual war out there. Just because you can't see the warring forces, doesn't mean they don't exist.

Peter was still feeling petulant. "Go on, fair knight. Fight the crusades and bring back some Saracen gold."

Peter was taken aback when John hugged him warmly.

"I've got all the gold I need right here with my family, thank you very much. Now remember, Pete, if you ever need anything, I'm still your older brother," John said.

Peter demurred and left the room, but not before John could notice the mist in his clear blue eyes.

Since finishing his education, John found a position as a history teacher in a Cedar Rapids high school. In addition to teaching and his duties in the Reserves, he was now happily married and consequently very occupied. Peter also joined the ROTC and, after a few false steps, eventually graduated. He had always been wild-spirited, and John always tried to steer his little brother in the right direction. Mercifully, working on the family farm seemed to temper him somewhat.

John's father, Anthony, had insisted that they all live together. He explained that there was plenty of room at the farm, and this was undoubtedly so. In addition to a five bedroom, two story, clapboard farmhouse, there were also 120 acres of corn and soybeans. He always said he'd seen enough of death and now he wanted to watch things grow. He was already an army chaplain now, having transcended the horrors of the Second World War. Being a man imbued with energy and a certain joie de vivre, he married late in life. His wife, Betty, would teasingly refer to him as her old man. She jokingly bemoaned her future state as a lonely widow. Ironically, it was she who preceded him to the grave, succumbing as she did to breast cancer.

Summer 2002

After the funeral, Anthony had become more reflective and would often engage in postprandial musings. Supper was a time for blessing food, home, and country. It was not a time for war stories. Once supper was finished, however, they would repair to the porch to enjoy the cool evening air. One night Mary pressed her father-in-law's broad shoulders, and he nodded his assent. The day had been long and she was exhausted and needed sleep. She was already six months pregnant. Anthony smiled wistfully as she parted and commenced.

"I was a marine on the USS El Dorado under General Simon Bruckner. Orders were given to disembark on L-Day. "L" stood for landing, which was scheduled for April 1, 1945. Yeah, I know, April's Fools Day. Anyhow, the place we were landing on turned out to be Okinawa, a 454 square mile island in southern Japan.

"The seventh and ninety-sixth divisions of the army and the first and sixth of the Marine Infantry landed on the southeast corner of the long, narrow island. We quickly occupied Hagushi, a village that gave access to two military airports. In three days we accomplished the occupation of these airports surprisingly without opposition. We quickly reached Ishikawa, the narrowest part of the island.

"Four days after landing, General Bruckner ordered the invading forces to simultaneously attack both ends of Okinawa. Marines covered the north and the army, the south. Once again, we were surprised to engage only a few Japanese soldiers. What we didn't know was that Lieutenant General Mitsuru Ushijima, who had fought in China and Burma, had hidden his troops in the south. And just like in Iwo Jima, their defenses were hidden underground. They had formidable weapons, such as the 320mm mortar. The Japanese numbered about 120,000 men. Many of these were veterans, willing to die in the name of the emperor. Their objective was to inflict as much damage as possible to the invading forces. The Japanese generals committed suicide in the manner of the samurais, rather than allow themselves to be taken as prisoners.

"Following eighty-three days of inferno on Earth after L-Day, the last defenses of the Japanese were defeated. More than 110,000 Japanese soldiers were killed. Almost 8,000 Americans were killed or missing in action. Some 4,000 marines died, and over 7,000 were injured as a result of kamikaze attacks.

"I observed the horror of fighting in a jungle infested with mosquitoes. I saw many of my fellow soldiers killed by the skillfully camouflaged Japanese. I vividly recall a Jeep with American soldiers in front of us stopping to let a couple of children cross the road. Just then, the children detonated their grenades, and the soldiers were ambushed by hidden machine gun fire. The sergeant in charge of our company gave the horrific order to shoot all civilians who approached our Jeeps. He didn't care if they were women, children, or the elderly. Can you imagine? From what I've heard, the same thing happened in Korea and Vietnam.

"Okinawa changed the course of the war. The Japanese finally became convinced that they were not invincible. That's what happened to Hitler after Stalingrad, and it proved to be a real game changer. In the United States, we had to minimize our losses. If Okinawa, with half a million inhabitants, cost so many lives, how many more would we lose fighting 110 million Japanese people across many islands?

"This all led to the atomic explosions in Hiroshima and Nagasaki. Though they killed many instantly, and later more still, they ended the war. The bombs had actually saved lives. It must be remembered that, in the German concentration camps and in the Russian Gulags, many more people died than in the two atomic explosions."

When the grim story ended, Anthony and his two sons hugged and went indoors. Little did they know that in due time, John and Peter Wagner would be notified that they would be part of their own military drama in Afghanistan.

*   *   *

As Abdullah was stirring in the cave, he noticed the play of light and shadow in the direction of the ditch where John was crouched trying to repair his weapon. He could not clearly see his American counterpart but nevertheless pondered the cause of the flickering lights. He snickered sardonically at his predicament. He was not accustomed to living under such straitened circumstances.

Abdullah Gul was the eldest son of a wealthy Afghan merchant. He grew up in a world of oriental opulence and travelled extensively throughout the Near East during vacations. Although his family had always been proud of his academic achievements, he had always felt a nagging curiosity regarding the West. He was not interested in hearing secondhand accounts demonizing a large portion of the globe. He could not help feeling mollycoddled growing up, and as a result decided to see things for himself when he finally came of age. He, therefore, went to London to study English, history, and computer science at the university level. He marveled at British society. He saw people from many different countries who were tourists, citizens, and students. Someone once commented to him that more languages could be heard throughout London than in any other city in the world. There were numerous stores, and a variety of clothing which allowed women to show their faces and expose their legs. It was like living in another universe, so different was it from home. Nevertheless, he admitted to himself, he found it all attractive, diverse, and enjoyable. He made friends with his fellow students, yet resisted the temptations of alcohol and partying.

He spent his weekends strolling through the parks and visiting the countryside where the pace of life was closer to that of home. He wondered, How, with such a diversity of people and customs, can there be peace, respect, and acceptance in society? He was astonished by buildings like

Buckingham Palace, with its daily ritual of the changing of the guards. He was bemused by the acceptance of the royal family, who were only nominally in charge of the British government. Another surprise was the freedom of expression he saw as he observed a group at Speakers Corner in Hyde Park. How can people improvise speeches and antigovernment rallies and remain unpunished? he wondered.

Within his university curriculum, his greatest difficulty lay with English. He responded to this challenge by working assiduously to overcome this shortcoming and made remarkable progress. Still, after three years living away from home, he decided it was time to return to Afghanistan. A job would be waiting for him there as a schoolteacher. Little did he know that his country would soon be at war and that an international military force would be fighting the Taliban across the country. Shortly after arriving home, he was recruited to a military corps where he ran a computerized communication center.

And now, he was reduced to living like a caveman. The ambient odor of the small, cold cave was vaguely familiar. Something like clay and freshly baked bread. Also there was the sharpness of the iron, which he remembered from servants pressing his family's clothes. He rummaged through his memories to find a match and smiled, childlike, when he found it. He was a mischievous boy and would often escape the watchful eyes of his minders. On one such occasion, he slipped into a potter's shop as the front door was ajar. Hidden by the shade, he never imagined he had been noticed by the old man immersed in his work.

"Come inside, *habibi*. I will not eat you."

Abdullah looked around the noisy, dusty street to see if anyone had noticed him. He knew his family would disapprove of a boy of his station being seen fraternizing with a tradesman. When he was satisfied that he had not been noticed, he tentatively entered the dimly lit room. The old man motioned him to sit as he resumed his work. His face was so finely lined in burnished ochre, that he resembled the handiworks he had neatly stacked around the room. Abdullah thought the man was a sort of snake charmer, as he saw the rising mass of clay take shape around the potter's wheel.

"That is magic," he finally said.

"Ah yes," the potter interjected. "There is magic in a man doing what's right for him."

"But why did you choose this trade instead of being a merchant? A merchant makes much more money and is well regarded."

The old man smiled. "This trade, as you call it, chose me. Why did you choose to be a little boy?"

"That's silly. I just am."

"Even so am I a potter."

Abdullah rose to leave and tried to look tall. "Yes. But tomorrow, I shall be a man."

The old man tittered. "By then, more than likely, I will be dead.

Abdullah's mood darkened. "That's so sad."

"Ah, no, habibi. It will be as if the coarsest clay were transformed by the heat of life into the finest porcelain."

Abdullah awakened from his reverie with a snap. What sentimental nonsense am I conjuring up when I should be steeling myself to face my enemy? he thought.

CHAPTER 3

Training for War in Afghanistan

John and Peter were engaged in basic training at an accelerated pace. They went through arduous training preparing to fight, carrying heavy backpacks and weapons. They marched in both hot and cold extremes, mimicking the wild swings in Afghan weather.

They were among the thousands of healthy, potentially successful members of a young generation. They could work to further develop a country already admired by many nations around the world. They were not told exactly when or for how long they would be away. They trained with Blacks, Hispanics, Asian-Americans, and American Indians, who were called Americans to perform their duty. Why? We all have the obligation of defending our homeland when attacked or threatened by other countries.

It was reasonable to fight the Japanese following the heinous attack on Pearl Harbor. It is understandable that the events of September 11, 2001 triggered feelings of hatred and revenge which precipitated the attack and defeat of Saddam Hussein and the Iraqi army. Disappointingly, the absence of weapons of mass destruction clearly indicated faulty intelligence.

Should we have paid more attention to the "reasons" for the 911 atrocities? We supported Saddam Hussein when Iraq went to war with Iran for eight years in the 1980s. We also trained and equipped the Taliban as well as Osama bin Laden when they fought the Soviets, only to later become their victims. Osama bin Laden had received CIA training. The United States has trained members of the Mexican police force to fight drug trafficking gangs in their country. The latter offered these forces higher pay, and many gang members switched bosses. Now they have joined the drug traffickers, fighting US agents and killing numerous civilians.

Osama bin Laden was born in 1957. He eventually became the leader of the terrorist organization known as Al Qaeda ("The Base"), which supports jihad in order to fight the "injustices" in the Arab world. To this end, this group condemns acts of fornication, homosexuality, and drug addiction. Al Qaeda accuses the US of raiding the natural resources of the Islamic world and supporting the enemies of Islam. No wonder the US hesitated in offering support to the rebels fighting Gaddafi in Libya. They were concerned with who will replace him. We must stop training potential enemies and spend more time and effort in preventing wars. As in medicine, prevention is more successful and cheaper than diagnostic tests and treatments.

The Taliban is an extremist group that originally took power in Afghanistan in 1996 and held it through 2001. They have oppressed and victimized women, who sometimes respond to the abuse by committing suicide. Their tribal confederation leader, Mullah Mohammed Omar, is still at large with a $25 million bounty for his capture. Between 1979 and 1989, the Afghans fought a war against the Soviet Union. The "mujadeen" (Islamic fundamentalists), were backed by the United States, as well as Saudi Arabia, Pakistan, and other Islamic countries. In 1979, the American Ambassador to Afghanistan was assassinated. Prime Minister Amin was also assassinated when the Soviet Army invaded the country that same year. The war effort was eventually abandoned by Mikhail Gorbachev, who ordered the retreat of the Soviet Army. This war has been called the Soviet Union's Vietnam.

The present war in Afghanistan started on October 7, 2001, with the United States and Great Britain comprising the stock of the International Security Assistance Force. It was a reaction to the assault on the United States on September 11. This force exercised Article 51 of the United Nations Charter which outlines the rights of nations to go to war to defend themselves. The objective was to capture Osama bin Laden, who assumed responsibility for the operation.

The Taliban is a fundamentalist Islamic militia established in 1995. The word means "students" in the Pashtun language. The ISAF is comprised of two military forces. The southern part of Afghanistan was primarily backed by the United States and forces in that region of the country and the east. The other force was established by the United States National Security Council with the purpose of stabilizing the government of Kabul and the surrounding areas. At one point there were 64,500 military people from 42 countries, of which the United States contributed about 30,000. The war escalated, and the ensuing surge resulted in the presence of more than 100,000 American troops. This war is now costing $116 billion dollars a year, not to mention the incredible loss of life.

Where was Osama bin Laden? He was eventually found and killed in Abbotabad, a military town in northern Pakistan, in May of 2011. He was 54 years old. It is important to remember that when leaders disappear, others take their place. It does not mean the end of the war. It is more important to educate, dialogue, and offer support than to try to oppose religious beliefs and political policies that the other party rejects. Respect, understanding, acceptance, and compromise are essential.

After training, John and Peter were shipped to Afghanistan. Officially known as the Islamic Republic of Afghanistan, the suffix -istan, meaning "land of," it is a central Asian nation comprising some 250,000 square miles in size. It gained its independence from Great Britain in August 1919. In its long history, this country has suffered invasions from Mongols, Persians, Arabs, Turks, Greeks, and, of course, Great Britain.

John and Peter's squadron flew to Kabul and joined the ground forces traveling southeast, bordering a mountain ridge. They were on a narrow road when the tragedy that took his brother struck. Rebel forces descended from the mountains in a well-orchestrated ambush. John could not save his brother, and though he was clearly injured, he felt it was a miracle he himself was able to escape alive.

CHAPTER 4

Dialogue between Two Enemies

John heard shots coming from a cave located somewhere above him, close to the base of the mountain. Twilight was approaching, and the blast furnace-like heat of the day was shifting into a cool breeze.

John shouted in desperation, "You bastards killed my only brother."

A voice was heard not too far from John. It was Abdullah shouting back, "You Americans are the real bastards who are destroying our beautiful country and trying to change our way of life."

John was surprised by Abdullah's command of the English language. He yelled again, "You savages killed my brother."

Abdullah responded, "Whoever you are, you are very good at projection. You people are the savages, killing and terrorizing defenseless civilians, including members of my own family who perished as a result of your barbarous raids." He scowled disdainfully. "Your so-called 'collateral damage.' As if a military euphemism could cover the terrible reality."

John winced. He remembered watching 60 Minutes a few years back when they were interviewing Madeleine Albright, President Bill Clinton's ambassador to the United Nations. When asked if the half-million children who died as a result of the corruption-tainted Oil-for-Food program had been worth it, she responded that though it was a hard choice, she thought it was worth it. To John this clearly illustrated the cavalier attitude the West took to the suffering of the people on the other side of the world. John had not only attended Sunday Mass, but had also gone to Sunday school. There he had been taught that we are all God's children. He felt himself pulled by the strain in Abdullah's voice.

After pausing a while, John said, "By dawn, one of us will be dead. Therefore, let us talk about ourselves and the war. You are a member of an extreme Islamic group, maybe 10 percent of Muslims, who are the product of the seeds of fanaticism and the call for jihad. In its mainstream form, Islam has its good principles. Mohammed promised eternal life, a sense of belonging, and he established one faith for one people. He introduced rules for getting along, brought order out of chaos, and most importantly abolished feuds and polytheism. But you have ignored these sacred precepts in your perverse attempts to use theology to justify your political aims."

Abdullah was taken aback by John's nuanced analysis. He therefore decided it would be a good idea to elaborate. "Islam is a way of life like Taoism is for some of the Chinese. We have six core beliefs. There is only one God. We believe in the prophets sent by God, in angels, and in the sacred books inspired by God—the Torah, the Gospels, and the Koran. We also believe in a judgment day and the resurrection of the dead, and finally in fate, whether good or bad."

"The five pillars of our religion are: First, Allah is the one God, and Mohammed is his prophet, though we also acknowledge other prophets such as Abraham, Moses, and Jesus. Second, pray five times a day facing Mecca in Saudi Arabia. This is our most sacred city, like Jerusalem is for the Christians and Jews. Third, be charitable or give alms to the poor. Fourth, fast during Ramadan, the ninth month of our calendar. And fifth, make the Hajj or pilgrimage to Mecca, which must be completed at least once in a lifetime."

"Our non-Muslim brothers do not know that the highest virtue is surrender or submission," he continued. "That is what Islam means: 'surrender to God.'"

John gesticulated toward the unseen speaker. "We Christians are also taught to submit to God's will. But who decides what is God's will? If you accept that Jesus was at least a prophet of God, why should his words have less weight than Mohammed's?"

Abdullah became excited. "Mohammed was the last prophet, and as such, his words have the stamp of finality."

John smiled and retorted, "My friend, we Christians have been collecting prophets all throughout history. Some have been called saints, sages, and holy men and women, with varying degrees of accuracy. Does chronology dictate the truth? I don't think so. The truth is both eternal and outside of time. Remember in John: 8:58, Jesus declares, 'Verily, verily, I say unto you. Before Abraham was, I am.' Rather than dwelling on our differences, let us reflect that both our peoples believe in God."

It must be realized that a great deal of Islamic doctrine evolved after the death of Mohammed. Likewise, the Christian Gospels were written after Jesus' crucifixion, and all the sixty-six books of the Bible were written by forty people over a span of 1,600 years (from 1513 BCE to 98 ACE). The Koran covers many varied subjects such as salvation, the apocalypse, war, and politics. It also addresses more mundane issues, such as the daily government of Medina and the collection of taxes.

Mohammed was born in the year 570 ACE, and he is considered by Islam as God's last prophet. Islam was born in the midst of turmoil much like Christianity, which flourished at a time when the Jews were dominated by the Romans and the basic principles of Judaism were in decline. When holy books like the Bible and Koran were translated into other languages, some statements were prone to errors and misinterpretations, which in turn leaves them subject to criticism. The words of God were not written by God. However, God has left his fingerprints and clues.

Muslims and Christians have both suffered from theological rifts. Muslims, following the death of Mohammed, witnessed a schism which resulted in the formation of two groups. Shias believe in Ali and the imams as successors to Mohammed, while Sunnis considers the first of four caliphs to be Mohammad's legitimate successor. Even up to the present day, these groups have been in conflict.

There are about 1.8 billion Muslims in the world, approximately 8 million in the United States. About 98 percent of Arabs are Muslims, however only 20 percent of Muslims are Arabs. The majority of Muslims are in Indonesia, Pakistan, and India, which are not Arab nations.

Christians in 1054 ACE experienced a rift between the Eastern Orthodox Church and the Western Roman

Catholic Church. Another rift came about in the sixteenth century during the Reformation, between the Roman Catholic Church and Protestant churches. The Protestants, in turn, have been fragmented throughout the world. Not too long ago, Catholics and Protestants waged a brutal war throughout Ireland. Consider that though the Hindus have many gods, other belief systems like Buddhism, Taoism, and Confucianism have no gods.

Among the Jews in Israel now, there is growing dissatisfaction with the ultra-orthodox known as haredin. The haredin are increasing in number and now represent 9 percent of the population. Though they do not serve in the army, only about 50 percent do any regular work. Sixty percent live in poverty. Though there are approximately 50,000 haredin in Israel today, by 2025 they may represent 15 percent of the population. Even among a traditionally oppressed and marginalized people, there are conflicts.

Having touched on some of these points as well as formally introducing themselves, John felt he should summarize. "Man has been at war since the beginning of his existence. Millions of human beings have died fighting for political and religious differences, ignoring the significance of our greatest treasure, which is life itself."

Abdullah reflected, "It is true. We are all brothers under the skin. We all originated from a group of about 10,000 early humans living in east Africa about 130,000 years ago. Despite the differences in our appearances and cultures, and the fact that sometimes we cannot even communicate with each other, we are all Allah's children. As such, we are blessed with a unique brain, capable of thoughts, feelings, and understanding."

John considered the academic nature of this exchange. How odd that one of them might be obligated to kill the other before long. Still, his conscience compelled him to comment, "We owe each other respect and consideration Each of us, no matter what our beliefs, could live peacefully, attempting to eradicate anger, resentment, jealousy, and fear. Hate and indifference should be replaced by love and caring."

Abdullah brightened. "Why, then, is the West trying to impose their culture and political views upon us?"

John sighed. "We are responding with war for the unnecessary and brutal killing of innocent civilians. Over 3,000 died and numerous others were injured in the September 11 attack on the Twin Towers in New York City."

Abdullah raised the index finger of his right hand. "Our right to jihad was the only way we could draw attention to the West, which has consistently ignored our right to peace, sovereignty, and world recognition. You Americans have killed many more than 3,000 innocent people in the wars with Iraq and Afghanistan, not to mention your unauthorized incursions into Pakistan. And don't forget, you Christians have had your own jihads in the form of Crusades and Inquisitions."

John nodded his assent. "It is important to settle our differences and learn forgiveness. Confucius said, 'Before you embark on a journey of revenge, dig two graves.' And Gandhi said, 'If we implement an eye for an eye, we should all be blind.' Forgiveness is very difficult and often comes at the cost of great suffering. We should think of the way the Jews use the word 'shalom.' It has been defined as the perfect, harmonious interdependence among all parts of creation."

CHAPTER 5

Encounter at Dawn

Dawn arrived. Abdullah ambled tentatively out of the cave. John had awakened to the looming sun, vaguely aware that the heat was gathering around him. However, due to weakness from his injuries, he once again lost consciousness. Abdullah approached him as the droning hum of armored vehicles filled the air like a distant thunder roll. He pounced on John and as he was preparing to kill him with his sword, John opened his eyes. He was physically unable to defend himself. Just then, a large cross around his neck reflected a piercing light. Abdullah lowered his sword, turned on his heels, and disappeared into the bushes.

Was this an act of forgiveness, dereliction of duty, or a miracle? What would be accomplished by killing an apparently good, well-educated man? Both of them became enemies by the orders of others. John didn't elect to be in

Afghanistan. Is war inevitable? Should we take a second look at the concept of implementing an eye for an eye? What good does it do to kill John when others would be sent in his stead with the same orders to search and destroy? Is there a viable substitute for war? Good, competent leaders of the world should sit around the table and discuss any lessons they may glean from their common history. They must operate from a bona fide desire to settle their differences through compromises, and not plan and execute wars. Why is the United Nations so unsuccessful in preventing wars? The number of soldiers and civilians who perished during the First and Second World Wars numbered in the millions. Are we close to a Third World War? How can we avoid it?

Abdullah was not a coward. His disobedience in not killing an enemy soldier was the result of his conviction that what he and John were doing was wrong. They both had families they treasured and wanted to live in peace. They had no wish or inclination to hurt and kill others. Sometimes circumstances trigger a response that is altogether disproportionate.

Jesus was encouraged to organize a military force to fight and vanquish the enemy. He refused. Instead he was tormented physically, emotionally, and mentally. When on the cross, He had the power to avoid the suffering inflicted on him and save himself. He did not. He forgave those who caused his misery. It is extremely difficult to emulate Jesus' reactions to temptation, injustice, suffering, and disappointment. Should we try to be more like Him and replace hatred with love, greed with charity, war with peace, sadness with joy, and selfishness with gratitude? Obviously, forgiveness is easier said than done.

Abdullah retreated to the mountains. He was exhausted physically and emotionally. He and John had discussed so much the previous evening! He had the ambivalent emotions of hatred and love, with the latter disguised by the cloak of forgiveness. He spent the day hiding, unable to continue fighting. When he finally rejoined his comrades, he asked to be allowed to return to his village. He explained that he needed time to recover from injuries inflicted by the enemy. His wish was granted. He had completely lost interest in pursuing a war he intellectually rejected. Was this transformation and the sparing of John's life an example of a miracle, something he had always heard about but never really believed? As the days progressed, his aggressiveness and hatred dissipated. He became patient, tolerant, and quiet. These changes soon became apparent to his wife and son. He wanted to start a new life outside the armed forces. He eventually became a teacher of English for children and adults. In his mind, he often recalled his conversation with John. He wondered what had happened to him.

CHAPTER 6

Rescue Mission which Saved John's Life

A small group of Alliance soldiers approached the ditch where once again John lay unconscious. He was the sole survivor of the ambush that claimed his brother's life. He was gently put on a stretcher and transported to a nearby military base. In addition to oxygen, painkillers, and sedatives, he was administered fluids through an IV. John had sustained a severe injury to his left leg. Amputation was considered. John vehemently protested and insisted on intensive therapy to save his leg. While lying in bed, he observed that many of his fellow comrades had sustained severe injuries. Some had lost their eyesight. Some had lost an extremity. Others had their heads wrapped in gauze, masking their traumas. And, naturally, there were those who ultimately lost their lives.

John observed many soldiers in a semicomatose state, who did not exhibit any external wounds. He inquired about the cause of this phenomenon, and learned these men had closed head injuries. John learned the meaning of TBI (traumatic brain injury). Many soldiers lay expressionless. Others ostensibly recovered, only to later suffer from CTE (chronic traumatic encephalopathy). It is related to some forms of dementia. It is estimated that that over 300,000 troops in Iraq and Afghanistan have suffered brain injuries. In the United States, TBI is the leading cause of death in children under the age of four. In soldiers, the mechanism manifests in rapid changes in atmospheric pressure from direct blows to the head from shrapnel. It has been coined the signature injury of Operation Iraqi Freedom. Headaches, dizziness, nausea, vomiting, and slurred speech may not appear for days or weeks after the injury. The brain suffers concussion, bleeding, edema, or diffuse axonal injury. Those who survive may suffer from depression, personality changes, impaired sensory perception, and cognitive and emotional disabilities (such as anxiety, phobias, or panic disorders).

Wars cause many costly deaths, but produce much more physical and psychological damage. Counting deaths alone, the costliest war in terms of American lives was the Civil War (1861-1865), with an estimated 618,625 deaths.

In the twentieth century, the death toll for Americans in World War I was over 117,000. In World War II, over 418,000 died, over 36,000 in the Korean War, and finally in the Vietnam War, over 58,000 Americans lost their lives. Most recently, in the twenty-first century, there have been over 3,000 deaths in Afghanistan, and over 5,000 deaths in Iraq. The number of wounded exceeds 40,000. In World War II alone, over 60 million people died worldwide. How many of the 2.3 million American veterans living today live a normal life is unknown. The number of wounded people, the psychological, social, and economic consequences of war, is indescribable.

In 87 war-torn countries, children are used as military forces, as reported by Theresa Betancourt in the Harvard Public Health Review, Fall 2011. She states that in Sierra Leone alone, after a brutal 11-year civil war, a survey of children revealed that over 70 percent had witnessed beatings, torture, maiming, and shootings. Over 60 percent had witnessed violent deaths, and had been beaten by soldiers. Some 50 percent reported having seen large-scale massacres. Thirty-nine percent have been regularly forced to take drugs, while 45 percent of girls and 5 percent of boys have been raped by their captors. Twenty-seven percent of these child soldiers have killed or injured others during the course of the war.

Not only in Iraq and Afghanistan, but in almost every war, children have been forced to witness unspeakable atrocities. In addition, the loss of their parents has exacerbated their emotional trauma. We have recently seen children being trained in the use of weapons in Afghanistan, Libya, Yemen, Palestine, and elsewhere around the world. Often pictures of American soldiers are used as targets. Adults have fostered hatred to members of other countries in many youngsters.

At first, John couldn't remember what had happened to him. He experienced the surreal sensation of living a nightmare, hearing noises where there was only silence. What had happened to his company? Where was Peter? He faintly recalled having a conversation with someone who spoke to him in English. Could this be real? Flashing images of an Afghan's face with piercing eyes full of hatred appeared in his dreams again and again. He sometimes woke up with a scream, anticipating death from a sword that never touched his body. After that, silence. Slowly, his mind cleared. He was informed about Peter. His body had been recovered. He then wondered, why was he still alive? Why was he spared from inevitable death? First from the IEDs and the hail of gunfire brought about during the ambush, and second from a rebel who easily overpowered and could have killed him. He could offer no resistance.

If what he remembered was true, John asked himself, why didn't Abdullah kill him? What happened to him? He asked his rescuers if they had seen a rebel, alive or dead, close to him. No one had seen Abdullah. When he told his story, they assumed he had been hallucinating.

CHAPTER 7

John's Rehabilitation in the United States

After a month at the military hospital, John was shipped stateside and admitted to the Walter Reed Army Medical Center in Washington, DC. There he remained convalescing for two weeks. His wounds had all healed, except his left leg and ankle, which required surgery and arthrodesis, or immobilization, of the ankle joint. From that point on, he was nagged by intermittent foot and ankle pain that forced him to walk with a limp.

John flew back to his home in Iowa to join Mary and Anthony. As he descended from the military vehicle and walked toward his family, there were tears rolling down his cheeks. John was thin and visibly aged as he limped toward his expectant loved ones. His wife and father took turns hugging him. They grabbed his duffel bag and helped him climb the stairs leading to the porch. They seemed completely happy, except for the haunting memory of mischievous Peter that brought forth the rising tears. It was unanimously decided the newborn would bear his dead uncle's name.

It took many days to listen to John's story. John insisted that only a miracle from God saved his life. Were there any lessons to be learned from the tragedy he had lived through? Both John and, especially, Anthony agreed that any war, no matter its motivation, should immediately cease and be replaced by negotiations aimed at providing peaceful coexistence.

John went to Sunday Mass and talked about his experience with his fellow parishioners. He wanted to reinforce his faith in the Lord. He was also interviewed on the radio and appeared on local TV stations. He told his story again and again, placing particular emphasis on his dialogue with Abdullah. He believed his experience was a message from God to seek peace where there is war.

One day, after services, Father Korb took him aside and asked him to speak at length the following Sunday. He would deliver his speech in lieu of the pastor's homily.

Somehow, that Sunday seemed different. Apart from the still, gelid air that seemed suspended in static expectation, the many birch trees loomed, their forlorn pallor giving the church grounds a vaguely funereal aspect. Though it was still autumn, it felt more like winter, only without the romantic embellishment of snow.

As the congregants wound their way up the flagstone walk and into St. Michael's Church, their muffled voices marked the gravity of the occasion. The echo of their shoes against the marble floor gave the odd sensation of an intricately designed mechanical clock. When the rustling of clothes finally settled in the pews, services began. Father Korb was a well-built, sturdy man of planter stock. His receding gray hair revealed a high forehead with deeply set gray eyes, betokening wisdom as well as native intelligence. The good father performed his pastoral duties admirably. This he did with a paternal solicitude that never degenerated into condescension. Part of his charm was his openness in allowing visiting ministers to deliver their own sermons. When it was time for the congenial pastor to give his homily, he motioned to John Wagner to speak in his stead.

As John walked, white-knuckling his cane with his right hand, he greeted the worshipers with a friendly nod. He had changed much from when they had seen him as a young student. His flaxen hair, already thinning in his early twenties, was now quite sparse indeed. This rather oddly gave him a somewhat childlike appearance. When he arrived at the lectern, he removed his spectacles from his tweed jacket along with some notes.

"I'm afraid, brothers and sisters, the man you find before you now is quite altered in appearance as well as in health. As you know, I have spoken at length of my experiences in Afghanistan. In particular, I have elaborated on the exchange I had with a fellow by the name of Abdullah Gul. This has changed the trajectory of my life for the better, which I have probably mentioned ad nauseum. It is not my intention now to reiterate what you have already heard, but rather to share with you the conclusions I have drawn. I humbly ask for your patience and forbearance."

There were scattered words of protestation that resolved into a low hum. John slowly raised his open palms and continued. "My brother, Peter, and I were sent to Afghanistan as part of the controversial surge that was supposed to overwhelm the Taliban. First of all, let me categorically state that we were very proud to serve our country and were quite prepared to die for it. Sadly, as you well know by now, my kid brother, in fact, did."

There followed a rumbling of commiseration that John patiently waited out.

"I have come to believe, however, that our military superiority, acknowledged throughout the world, is not the cure for the ills of an increasingly interdependent world.

There are times, my friends, when what is called upon instead is perhaps our moral superiority. Not to any of our enemies, mind you, but to what is basest in ourselves. We are called upon to live by the noble ideals that founded this great nation and not the thuggery of the idea that might makes right.

"It is true, we were attacked by Islamic terrorists on September 11, 2001. However, now that we have brought Osama bin Laden, the mastermind behind the attack, to justice, what justifies our continued presence in Afghanistan? Certainly, for the moment, we must remain there to stabilize the country, but our resources should now be concentrated on infrastructure and medical care. We must win the hearts of the people and not demonize ourselves, and thus play into our enemies' hands. Only then will they be unwilling to wage jihad against a country that holds no ill will toward them. My friends, there are rogue nations throughout this globe too numerous to mention. Are we to be in a state of perpetual conflict, bankrupting our country both morally and financially? I ask you to reflect that our former enemy Vietnam is now one of our closest allies in the Far East.

"The war we must win is a moral one. Luckily, America has always been a moral country founded on sound Judeo-Christian precepts. She cannot allow herself to be warped by the perverse motives driving the Islamic extremists. By depriving these elements of any moral rationale to commit jihad, we eliminate their very raison d'etre.

I am not suggesting we adopt a pie-in-the-sky or Polyanna attitude toward terrorism or terrorists. What I am advocating instead is that we help the people who these terrorists wish to manipulate for their own bloody purposes. As we have seen, the terrorist as such is a selfish narcissist. Therefore, any dealings with them smacks of appeasement and blackmail. We must instead engage with the more moderate leaders in Afghanistan and Iraq, to try to establish a workable rapprochement for our mutual welfare. We must offer them incentives to cooperate with our efforts to modernize their countries. They, in their turn, must respond with peace and goodwill. And always, as President Reagan suggested when dealing with the Soviets, 'trust but verify.' We must establish an atmosphere of mutual trust and respect, realizing always that every nation on earth merits their own autonomy. If, at the conclusion of our agreed upon stay in Afghanistan, their peoples should decide by referendum that we must leave, we have to respect their wishes. These countries should realize that through our shared trials and tribulations, we will always enjoy a unique relationship. Therefore, there can be no ignominy in requesting each other's assistance should the need arise. Hopefully, though we've had to live through the disgrace of Abu Ghraib and other demeaning abuses in Guantanamo, we have reached a stage of entente as opposed to détente. This is no small task given the widely divergent histories of our countries. Quite the contrary, it was our very differences that Al Qaeda, and to a much lesser extent the Taliban, counted on to drive a wedge between us. Perhaps we may yet reach an agreement with the Taliban and convince them to respect the will of their own people. We have no intention of occupying Afghanistan. Indeed, as history has shown, it is probably impossible to do so.

"As concerns Al Qaeda, however, I am under no illusion. Their sole purpose is to destroy the West and possibly all of Christendom. They represent no country as such, but rather serve as a sort of criminal gang, exploiting the collective hatred and frustration of a marginalized population. Luckily, they represent a minority of the population. This, of course, does not mean they are not dangerous. Their very existence is anathema to the West and Israel, and as such they must be brought to justice. We will not succeed in eliminating this element from any country, any more than we can succeed in eliminating criminals from our world. They are everywhere, and, yes, sadly, they are even here in our beloved homeland. We must increase our intelligence resources, hire more trained linguists, and infiltrate their ranks wherever they operate. In short, we must treat them like the common criminals that they are. Al Qaeda has informed us that we in the West love life whereas they love death. Since they are motivated by the prospect of future rewards in paradise, their actions are not ethical. Rather, by this sordid self-interest, the terrorist's actions are degrading, or at the very least questionable. A terrorist is possessed of a sick, misanthropic rage which views the silly, callow, West as Al Qaeda's whipping boy. He desires to make our entire civilization a scapegoat that will purge him of sin, and in the process elevate himself. In a final irony, the suicide bomber, who after all is the jihadist par excellence, attempts to usurp God's role as final arbiter, and in an act of mad destruction, endeavors to become Creator and sacrifice simultaneously. The puritanical jihadist, by acting with such hubris, thus blasphemes the very God he claims to worship.

"Brothers and sisters, I am not proposing that we negotiate with these deranged people. Instead, I propose that we engage with the legitimate leaders of the nations of the world in good faith.

"As you know, the sacrifice that must be made to purge a sinful humanity has already been made by our Lord Jesus Christ. He had the sole legitimacy to make of himself a blessed sacrifice that we should inherit the grace we enjoy therein. No hate-driven terrorist, through whatever specious motives he may have, can offer the same. The terrorist is befouled and delusional. He certainly holds no mandate from God.

"It should be remembered that God the Father did not torture Jesus during his passion, rather the religious and civil authorities punished this human reflection of the Almighty. This distortion is something we should bear in mind. You see, we are all in danger of succumbing to our baser impulses under the justification of religion. We would, therefore, be wise as well as pious to heed Jesus' very words in his Sermon on the Mount. Let us turn to the familiar words in Matthew 5: 43-48.

"'Ye have heard that it hath been said, "Thou shalt love thy neighbor, and hate thine enemy." But I say unto you, Love your enemies, bless them that curse you, do good to them that hate you, and pray for them that despitefully use you, and persecute you; That ye may be the children of your Father which is in heaven; for he maketh his sun to rise on the evil and on the good, and sendeth rain on the just and on the unjust. For if ye love them which love you, What reward have ye? Do not even the publicans the same? And if ye salute your brother only, What do ye more than others? Do not even the publicans so? Be ye therefore perfect, even as your Father which is in heaven is perfect.'

"I do not pretend that I adhere strictly enough to the divine words of the Lord, friends, but I put to you that as Christians, we must make more of an effort. In the same way we must not turn our backs on the homeless and needy in our community, we cannot afford to ignore those who suffer throughout our world. There are countries in this world that have legitimate needs we should address. Not just the United States should do this, naturally, but all those who are affluent enough. It must also be remembered that help can be offered in many forms, including expertise and knowledge. Please direct your attention to Matthew 25: 34-40.

"'Then shall the King say unto them on his right hand. "Come ye blessed of my Father, inherit the kingdom prepared for you from the foundation of the world; For I was hungry and you gave me meat; I was thirsty, and ye gave me drink; I was a stranger and ye took me in; Naked and ye clothed me; I was sick and ye visited me; I was in prison, and ye came unto me." Then shall the righteous answer him, saying, "Lord, when saw we thee hungry, and fed thee? Or thirsty, and gave thee drink? When saw we thee a stranger, and took thee in? Or naked, and clothed thee? Or when saw we thee sick, or in prison, and came unto thee?" And the King shall answer and say unto them, "Verily I say unto you, inasmuch as you have done it unto one of the least of these my brethren, ye have done it unto me."

"Staying with Matthew, recall the Pharisee lawyer asking Jesus which is the great commandment. To which Jesus responds in Matthew 22: 37-40.

"'Jesus said unto him, "Thou shall love the Lord thy God with all thy heart, and with all thy soul, and with all thy mind. This is the first and great commandment. And the second is like unto it, Thou shalt love thy neighbor as thyself. On these two commandments hang all the law and the prophets.'

"In the end as we have seen, when we love others, we are also loving God. If we are made in God's image, this suggests that we are capable of much more love than we are expressing. Remember, brothers and sisters, God created us ex nihilo, out of nothing. It was through his infinite grace that we were granted life with all its infinite possibilities. It behooves us, therefore, to respond to this divine gift with gratitude and also humility. When we truly see our fellow men and women as our brethren and kin, we must surely arrive at the conclusion that violence is not the means by which we must resolve our conflicts. We must humbly ask our Lord and Creator to inspire us with peaceful and rational solutions to the problems facing us today. We must be a beacon of righteousness for the world to see, so that indeed they shall know us by our fruits. Thank you, brothers and sisters, for your time, and may God bless you all."

The congregants shot glances at each other, and coming to an understanding rose in thunderous applause.

That night, as John and his family were enjoying their traditional roast beef dinner, he made an announcement. "Dad, Mary, I've been meditating for a while on the reason I was sent to Afghanistan and what possible lessons I may have learned. For instance, why was Peter killed and I spared? We were right next to each other. Then the next morning, instead of killing me, Abdullah heads for the hills. Why? It doesn't make sense."

Anthony cleared his throat. "Son, you are clearly suffering from survivor's guilt, which is perfectly natural given the circumstances. However, please realize that God's ways are ineffable. Peter has been taken to a far better place where perhaps he can finally find some peace."

Mary smiled. "And I can feel his namesake kicking in agreement."

John rubbed her swollen belly. "Go easy on your mom, sport." He became serious again. "Please understand, I'm grateful to be alive, and I'm not complaining. I wouldn't switch lives with anyone. What I am saying is that I want to make a difference in the way this country is run. I love teaching kids, but I feel I have got to get directly involved.

When I first began teaching history and government, I deceived myself into believing the kids were truly involved. Now I realize they are totally tuned out, obsessed with their own virtual fantasies. I've given this a lot of thought, and I decided to seek the seat being vacated by our retiring representative, Charles Wellesley."

Mary shot a glance at her father-in-law before turning to John. "Honey, with the baby due in a little bit, do you really think we could afford it?"

Anthony dismissed the thought. "Of course we can afford it. I have my savings and some money came to me from your mother's folks when she passed away. If John wishes to take an active role in government, I would like to encourage him. What we need is more men and women of integrity in Congress."

John waved his hands in protest. "Mary, I understand your concerns. I was thinking I could test the waters during the summer vacation. I already have some name recognition, and if I fail to gain traction, no harm done."

Anthony merrily slapped John's back. "Nonsense, son. You're a shoo-in. Just remember the astute observation of the late, great Speaker of the House Tip O' Neill, who said, 'You can get a lot done in government if you are willing to let other people take the credit.'"

CHAPTER 8

John Considers a New
Political Career

When John Wagner assumed his seat as an Independent in the House of Representatives, everyone was surprised, except possibly his father. John insisted on running as an Independent because he was wary of any restraints the two major parties might impose on him. Being an Independent allowed him to frequently cross the aisles to work on touchy partisan issues. He sat with the Democrats solely because the Republicans, at first, ostracized him. Charles Wellesley had been a conservative Republican of the finest mint.

The Republican candidate for a Wellesley's seat was Chester Smith, a doddering old demagogue who had been a mayor of one of Iowa's smaller rural towns. He was ill at ease in front of the bright lights and camera lenses of national politics. John Wagner easily defeated Smith as well as the Democratic challenger. It was reported in some news media, that some Republicans sighed in guilty relief at Chester's loss. The very dignity of the great state of Iowa was at stake. Some of the more jaded critics claimed that in addition to assuming his former post as mayor, Chester supplemented his income by selling his locally famous or infamous Mountain Cool Water, concocted in his privately owned stills. No one knew the origins of the name though, as Iowa is essentially flat.

John had attained something of the status of a folk hero through his appearances in local media and in person at state fairs and parades. His qualifications were his honesty, integrity, and compassion. He was a tireless scholar who thoroughly studied each issue before taking a stand. In addition, he was an injured soldier who bore marks of the wounds he suffered at war.

What some assumed was a liability was, in fact, an asset. John's nonpartisan approach to the nonstop debates on the House floor allowed him to adopt a more nuanced stance to the issues. He owed no allegiance to either party, and as a result was able to vote with his conscience. This won him kudos from both colleagues and the press. It was not long before he was asked to deliver commencement speeches at small colleges throughout the state, leading up to an engagement in his own alma mater, the University of

Iowa. John used all this free publicity to parlay a win at the open Senate seat after just two House terms. The Senate, with its reputation for restraint and gravitas, suited John far more than the noisy politicking the lower chamber was notorious for.

Once again, his ability to negotiate the often turbulent waters of the bipartisan Senate earned him a begrudging respect even as a junior senator. He, of course, never mentioned that when he returned to Iowa in Senate recesses, in addition to paying careful attention to the concerns of his constituents, he would consult with his wise and learned father. Naturally, when he would speak at the Senate floor, his speeches were imbued with some of that very same wisdom. It was a simple process of osmosis. In due time, John was assigned to the Senate's Foreign Relations Committee. Now the hard work would begin in earnest.

CHAPTER 9

John's Performance in Congress

When Chad Collins approached Senator Wagner asking for a position on his staff, he was immediately hired. It was rather like asking your favorite uncle for a summer job. Chad had been something of a protégé when he was a student in John's government class. In addition to ranking at the top of his class academically, he would always volunteer to do any extra credit work. Therefore, when John heard that Chad had graduated from Georgetown at the top of his class, he was not surprised. Chad had always been precocious, and some of his peers felt a tad too serious behind his horn-rimmed glasses. John knew that Chad's reserved façade masked a compassionate and earnest nature.

Chad appeared in his office laden with files of pending legislation. "Sir, I realize that you are very busy. But I would like to discuss some pending legislation with you that I feel has been drafted ambiguously for all too obvious reasons."

John smiled proudly. "Chad, I fear your days of sleepless, laborious study are not quite at an end. In fact, I fear they have just begun. You may well rue the day you asked me for employment, my boy."

"Sir, I consider it an honor."

"Please Chad, don't address me as 'sir' or 'senator.' My name is John. I want you to feel as if you are my junior partner. I bring this up for very practical reasons, without any thought to any protocols of etiquette. I need you to help me draft some sensitive legislation that is of vital importance in international relations."

"Yes, sir—I mean, John." Chad blushed. "I'm sorry, I know what you mean. I've been working diligently on your conflict resolution bill. We must be extremely careful with the wording so that it does not get sidetracked to some irrelevant committee where it will be missing in action, so to speak. We must not allow the opposition to muddy the waters with surrogate issues."

"Yes." John became pensive. "I must have a draft ready to deliver to the Senate floor by next week. We must get this done prior to the winter recess. Get your crew to work on this post-haste. And Chad, I'm counting on you."

"Consider it done, John." Chad saluted his boss with a nod and left.

John reflected on what Chad had said. The Senate was becoming increasingly contentious. Each day it reminded him more and more of the carnival atmosphere and horse trading so common in the House of Representatives. How was it the Foreign Relations Committee never addressed the irregularities manifested clearly in the Abu Ghraib scandal? he wondered. Why had they acted so expeditiously in the Terry Schiavo case? Was that just politicking? He hoped not. Still, it was remarkable with what solidarity they had enacted in 2005 the bankruptcy 'reform' so popular with the credit card companies. He tried desperately not to be tainted by the rampant cynicism endemic in Washington and, to a larger extent, the halls of congress.

He remembered an article he had read in the past concerning the astronaut Edgar Mitchell. How on returning to Earth from space, he had seen our fragile planet traveling precariously in a vast universe. How he came to feel a oneness with everything and everyone. How he noticed that from space, no artificial man-made borders were discernible. Nor was he aware of any differences between himself and any other man due solely to skin color, culture, or religion. This phenomenon has become known as the overview effect, and scientists have studied it extensively. Mitchell had even established the Institute of Noetic Sciences (IONS) to further investigate this fascinating phenomenon. Needless to say, this experience had completely changed his life for the better. Of course, jettisoning the entire Senate out of Earth's gravitational field would be a rather impossible thing to do. Still, he wished his fellow senators would display more camaraderie and cooperation, especially on the more important issues. By extension, he wished the same for the often obstreperous ambassadors that made up the General Assembly of the United Nations. Only by truly seeing the interconnectedness of man could global problems be solved. This was the reason John had sought a seat in the Senate in the first place. Sometimes bringing together partisans from both sides of the aisles made him felt like he was the only adult in the chamber, so childish could these grown men and women be.

CHAPTER 10

Outline of a Conflict Resolution Bill

When Senator Wagner's conflict resolution bill finally came up for a vote, it turned out not to be completely without precedent. During the 1920s, advocates for the League of Nations proposed the establishment of a World Court. William E. Borah, the Chairman of the Foreign Relations Committee at the time, went one better. The ever-grandiloquent and charming senator proposed instead a bill outlawing war. On January 15, 1929, the treaty passed the Senate 85 to 1. This was quite remarkable, given that there were not 50 states in the Union at the time, and consequently, the Senate did not have 100 members as it has today.

As it was, Senator Wagner's bill did eventually pass by a vote of 72 to 18 with 10 senators abstaining. It quickly was approved by the House of Representatives and was signed into law by the President of the United States.

The highlights of the bill were:

1) Immediately stop air raids and ground attacks.

2) Return ground troops and airplanes to bases in Afghanistan and other neighboring countries.

3) Select an American team to negotiate with Afghans who have lived in the United States and are familiar with both cultures.

4) Offer assistance particularly in two important areas: health and education.

5) Create a health program which would offer on-site (in various Afghan communities) primary and specialty health services, using the direct participation of physicians from the United States and other participating countries, with emphasis on telemedicine.

6) Mandate for the extensive use of nursing and public health personnel.

7) Send personnel fluent in the various Afghan languages to communicate directly with the population and to serve as translators.

8) Supply vaccines and basic medications free of charge.

9) Offer training to Afghans in graduate and postgraduate programs in the United States and in other participating countries, with emphasis on health and basic education programs.

10) Assist in the restoration of damaged roads and electrical installations, as well as other public services.

11) Exchange personnel in all areas of services to the public at large (i.e., training in and outside Afghanistan, health care and educational services).

12) Support the government in helping its people and emphasize the importance of order for their people's stability and long-lasting peaceful existence.

13) Respect the culture and offer assistance only when requested.

14) Allow peaceful protests.

In summary, the bill said that the United States will offer governments with which it is currently at war international help, particularly in the areas of health, education, and financial aid to rebuild their economies.

It also said that the United States and the members of ISAF will also exchange weapons of war for tools of peace. Immediate meetings would take place among individuals from the East (particularly Afghans) and Western countries.

Having resolved these domestic affairs, John turned his attention to the United Nations. He had long been skeptical of the efficacy of that particular institution. Another consideration that he had to negotiate with the US Ambassador to the UN, was the internationalization of this primarily American law. When they had crafted a working model, John presented his plan to effectively pass it through the UN. He also shared some of his misgivings concerning the poor management of that institution.

In 1947, when Trygve Lie was the first Secretary-General, the entire UN staff comprised 1,200 people. Since then, the ranks have swollen exponentially. According to the Congressional Research Service (CRS), Kofi Annan reduced the current level from 12,000 to fewer than 9,000. However, the Wall Street Journal points out that the bloated staff of the secretariat has grown to more than 17,000. Let us hope that Ban Ki-moon does a better job economizing.

In Post Tziporen, along the Israeli-Lebanese border, there are two flags clearly visible. One is the familiar blue flag of the United Nations. The other is the yellow Hezbollah one with the AK-47 prominently displayed in the background. The symbolism is at best ambiguous. The UN does not seem to be an honest broker in quelling violent uprisings.

When the Cash-for-Food program was initiated under the auspices of the UN, Saddam Hussein was able to skim billions to buy Security Council votes and bribe politicians. The little food that was allowed to reach the Iraqi people was reported to not be fit for swine feed. Following the 1995 Security Council Resolution 986, 17 charters from the Security Council to enforce Iraqi disarmament were all for naught. The one billion dollars allowed every 90 days for humanitarian purposes produced only subpar medical equipment and supplies. The Baghdad office supervising the operations was mostly staffed by Iraqis.

When the Iraqi Governing Council hired the Ronald Berger Strategy Consultants to audit the books, they estimated that no less than 10 percent of the Cash-for-Food funds went directly to Saddam Hussein. The countries benefitting mostly from the subprime oil prices that this program featured were two dependable opponants of US policy, France and Russia. It is interesting that France, so reluctant to act on behalf of its ally, the US, was quite eager to engage oil-rich Libya.

It must be remembered that in 2002, all of France was agog over the Thierry Meyssan bestseller L'Effroyable imposture. This roughly translates to "the Appalling Imposture" or "the Appalling Sham." In this book, M. Meyssan claims the 9/11 attacks on the World Trade Center and the Pentagon were orchestrated by the latter. Apparently, the planes that hit the towers were remote-controlled and the Pentagon was damaged by explosives planted on the ground. With friends like these in the Security Council, one must be guarded in one's approach.

The United Nations is a bloated bureaucracy that has largely become irrelevant because it works at cross-purposes. There is no cooperation for global projects initiated by the United States, despite the fact that the US pays $7 billion a year to keep it functioning.

No. No. For Senator Wagner's money, he would put his faith on what he called the Coalition of Responsible Engagement (CORE). This he modeled after President George W. Bush's Proliferation Security Initiative. It would include France amongst its members, how could it not? But it would also include more reliable allies like Australia, Japan, Poland, Portugal, Spain, the United Kingdom, Germany, the Netherlands, and Italy. When the initial trial run, as it were, had run its course, the General Assembly of the United Nations expressed interest and outrage that their nations were not included. This new development, of course, was warmly welcome by the majority of this organization, and the CORE principles were clearly delineated by the US Ambassador to the United Nations. It contained language that described the steps necessary to end any current wars and most importantly, to prevent future conflicts with other nations.

CHAPTER 11

John Returns to Afghanistan

Senator John Wagner headed a peace commission which visited Afghanistan. He was accompanied by other members of Congress, some Afghan professionals, and diplomats and representatives from the United Kingdom, Canada, Australia, Israel, France, Germany, China, India, Russia, and other countries, many from the Arab world. The tactic of using the CORE countries' union to pressure the United Nations had worked successfully. Countries that would not normally cooperate in collective diplomatic missions were now found in lockstep with each other.

They were to meet as a large committee first, then subsequently in smaller groups with representatives of the Afghan government, the Taliban, and any other guerrilla groups. In the beginning, tension and uneasy feelings prevailed among all the parties involved. The American delegation brought small gifts and a large banner with a three-dimensional rendition of the world. The flags of every nation were displayed. The statement "all for one, and one for all" appeared in the lower border of the banner. The following statement was included: "We brothers living in this unique planet pledge to help each other by treating everyone with love, charity, and respect during our shared existence."

Music and dancing were made available by the local host, for all those who wished to participate. The seating arrangements placed Americans next to Taliban leaders. Arguments and recriminations were not permitted. What hostilities they experienced between them should remain in the past, and they should learn from their mistakes—mistakes they pledged never to repeat.

A week after the arrival of John and his delegation, John requested to be driven to the site of his rescue. He and a group of soldiers travel on dusty and seemingly trackless terrain. However, through his Humvee's global positioning system, he was able to find the ditch where he spent a memorable night dialoguing with Abdullah. He motioned to his men to give him some alone time.

Once he found the correct spot, he knelt, prayed, and thanked God for being alive. As he rose, he saw a whirlwind of ochre dust gathering around him. He covered his eyes and crouched close to the ground. When the storm had passed, he found to his amazement a charm with Arabic script lying on the ground. He knew that Muslims were expected to be able to read the Koran in its native Arabic. Therefore, he felt optimistic about finding someone to translate it for him. He boarded the Humvee, and they retraced their steps.

He felt drawn to a small village on the way back to Kabul and ordered his driver to stop. He noticed some children walking toward what appeared to be a school. He followed them into a room filled with Afghan children. He asked if there was anyone who could speak English, but they only smiled shyly.

Just then, he heard the sound of robust laughter, and a man greeted him in impeccable English. His voice was familiar. John looked intently into his eyes and immediately recognized Abdullah Gul. As they embraced, they could not contain their tears. So much had happened to them. Though they came from opposite sides of the world, they felt like brothers. After regaining his composure, John extended the charm to Abdullah, who gently took it in his hands.

After reading it, he asked John, "Where did you find this?" It was a rhetorical question. He did not expect an answer, but instead seemed perplexed by the serendipitous nature of John's discovery. John smiled, as he could clearly see Abdullah's reaction was positive.

"Could you tell me what it means?"

Abdullah read the script aloud and replied softly, "It means 'peace.'"

Synopsis

The Dialogue in Afghanistan graphically illustrates the horrors of war and proposes cogent and rational alternatives to conflict resolution.

The purpose of The Dialogue is to clearly delineate self-explanatory, a priori truths concerning the nature of war in an accessible and readable manner. The protagonist, John Wagner, is an everyman figure who will be readily identifiable to all readers. Given the abbreviated format of the pocket book, the narrative is fast-paced and urgent.

From the opening scene, we are transported from purely technical matters to the experience of John's personal loss (i.e., the death of his brother). This serves the purpose of characterizing the imperative nature of solving the problem of war. Rarely do we fully comprehend the complexity of any phenomenon until it touches us directly.

Later, in the chapter that gives the book its name, arguments are offered to explain the origins and nature of war. Here, emphasis is placed on its historical and cultural pedigree. It is important to note that violent conflict is not an innate attribute of man, and thus need not imprison or define him.

Throughout the book, the negative effects of war are exhaustively reported. The medical repercussions are set forth with clinical accuracy. It is important that the reader is kept aware at all times of the ramifications of this state-sponsored act of recklessness. He must not be lulled into a false sense of security, or made to feel that all the chaos is being enacted "over there." The corrosive effects of war affect us all.

In the passage where a chastened John Wagner speaks before the congregation of his church, a uniquely Christian perspective is given to the issue of conflict resolution. However, the underlying message is one that resonates with people of all faiths.

Arguments are made in favor of rational polemic in lieu of fiery rhetoric and cultural bias. War is defined as the final option, and, frankly put, a failure to effect reasonable diplomatic negotiations. We must propose a model whereby might is not necessarily right, and mutual respect prevails.

Only then can all parties feel that they are equally invested in the endeavor to achieve world peace.

The book proposes possible reasons for our current war in Afghanistan. The rationale behind the presence of the International Security Assistance Force (ISAF) in Afghanistan is also addressed, as well as the cultural indoctrination that makes a respectful discussion amongst peers well-nigh impossible. Only when we cease to measure others by our standards can differences in religion, culture, economics, and political life be addressed. It is argued that if an entente cannot be reached, at the very least, a detente should be possible.

When people around the world value human life equally, diplomacy can be conducted on a level playing field. The unacceptability of "collateral damage" as a justification for brutality and carnage is also noted. A curious idiosyncrasy of human behavior dictates that the more you abuse "the enemy," the more you grow to hate and despise him. This phenomenon, reminiscent of the Holocaust, must not be casually brushed aside. Mutual respect is, therefore, in the best interest of everyone.

What is ultimately demonstrated by the author is the futility of war. Human history clearly shows the cyclical nature of human conflicts. It is this very fact that makes of war a self-perpetuating and endless drama. It is a drama that has cost millions of human lives since its incipience.

The author proposes a cogent, effective plan to rid this world of this scourge. Given the limitations of the pocket book format, this work, perforce, will give the reader the impression of a modern day morality play. It is the very universality of its archetypal elements that make this work so relevant today.